Adapted by Teddy Slater

Illustrated by Ric Gonzalez and Ron Dias

A GOLDEN BOOK • NEW YORK

Copyright © 1997, 2004, 2010 Disney Enterprises, Inc. All rights reserved. Published in the United States by Golden Books, an imprint of Random House Children's Books, a division of Random House, Inc., 1745 Broadway, New York, NY 10019, and in Canada by Random House of Canada Limited, Toronto, in conjunction with Disney Enterprises, Inc. Golden Books, A Golden Book, A Little Golden Book, the G colophon, and the distinctive gold spine are registered trademarks of Random House, Inc.

www.randomhouse.com/kids

Library of Congress Control Number: 2003105378

ISBN: 978-0-7364-2197-3

Printed in the United States of America

40

Once upon a time there lived a young prince in a beautiful castle. Although he had everything his heart desired, the prince was spoiled and selfish.

One winter's night, an old beggar woman asked the prince for shelter from the cold. In return she offered him a rose. Repulsed by the old woman, the unkind prince turned her away.

The woman warned him not to be deceived by appearances, since beauty is found within. When the prince dismissed her again, the old woman's ugliness melted away to reveal a beautiful enchantress.

The prince tried to apologize, but it was too late. The enchantress knew there was no love in his heart.

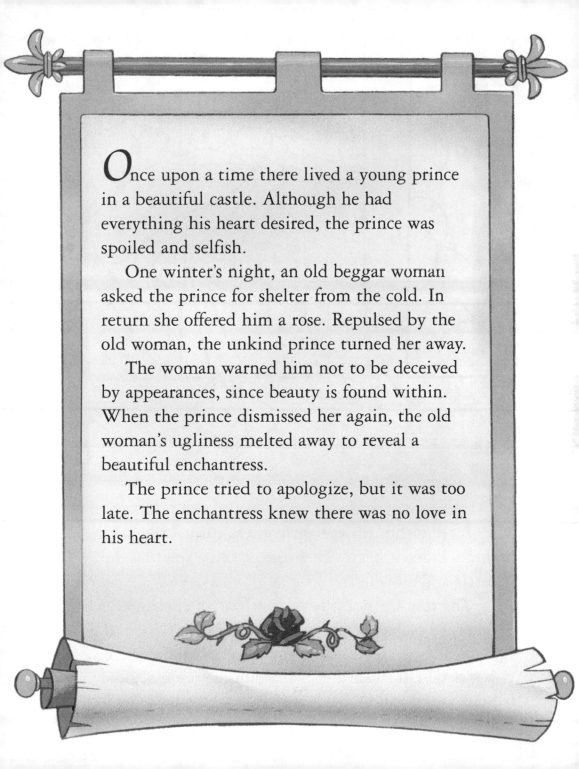

As punishment, the enchantress turned the prince into a hideous beast. Then she placed a spell on the castle and all who lived there.

The rose she had offered him was an enchanted rose. It would bloom until the prince was twenty-one. If he could learn to love and be loved in return before the last petal fell, then the spell would be broken. If not, he would remain a beast forever.

Ashamed of his monstrous form, the Beast hid inside the castle. A magic mirror was his only window to the outside world.

As the years passed, he fell into despair. Slowly the rose began to wither. He did not believe anyone could ever love him.

In a nearby village there lived a beautiful young woman named Belle. Belle, unlike the other girls in the village, cared only for her books. She always felt out of place.

Belle loved to read about adventure and romance. Her father, Maurice, loved books, too. Maurice was an inventor—a genius, according to Belle; a crackpot, according to the townsfolk.

"Belle is even stranger than her father," the villagers whispered. "Her nose is always in a book, and her head is in the clouds."

Gaston, the handsomest man in town, wanted to make Belle his wife. Even though she thought he was a brainless brute and turned him down again and again, Gaston was determined to wed the lovely Belle.

One cold day Maurice hitched his horse, Phillipe, to a wagon and set off to show his latest invention at a faraway fair.

But Maurice read the map wrong and became lost in a forest. As an icy wind whistled through the trees, he suddenly heard the howling of wolves! Phillipe bolted, and Maurice fell to the ground. Trying to escape the wolves, the frightened man ran deeper and deeper into the woods.

He came to a castle and stumbled inside. There he was greeted by Mrs. Potts the teapot, Cogsworth the clock, and Lumiere the candelabrum, who had all been servants to the prince. But before he had time to marvel over these strange creatures, an even stranger one appeared—the Beast!

When Maurice stared in horror, the Beast howled angrily. Then he scooped Maurice up and carried him off to a dungeon.

Meanwhile, Phillipe had made his way back home.
Belle took one look at the riderless horse and knew
something awful had happened to her father.

"Phillipe! Take me to him!" she cried, leaping into
the horse's saddle. Without a pause, Phillipe thundered
off toward the woods.

When they reached the castle, Belle burst inside and
searched frantically for her father. The enchanted
objects led her to the dungeon, but just as she found
Maurice, the Beast appeared. Belle let out a terrified
gasp at the sight of the hideous creature.

She begged the Beast to free her father. When he
refused, she bravely offered to take Maurice's place.

"No, Belle!" Maurice cried, but the Beast agreed to
the exchange.

Before Belle could bid her father good-bye, the Beast
led her to her room. "The castle is now your home," he
said gruffly. Belle was free to go anywhere she liked—
except the West Wing.

"You will join me for dinner," the Beast ordered.
"That's not a request."

Still, Belle refused, and the Beast stomped off in anger.

That night Belle slipped out of her room and found her way to the forbidden West Wing.

There she saw the enchanted rose by the window. When she reached out to touch it, the Beast suddenly appeared on the balcony outside the window.

Belle screamed and fled from the room.

Her heart pounding, Belle ran out of the castle, mounted Phillipe, and galloped off into the night. But a pack of wolves soon had them surrounded. Belle was helpless.

Suddenly the Beast was there, throwing the wolves aside. Belle heard terrible snarling and howling as the Beast and the wolves battled for their lives. At last the wolves ran off into the woods, but the Beast lay in the snow, badly injured.

Back at the castle, Belle carefully tended to the Beast's
wounds. Gentle as she was, the Beast roared in agony.

"I barely touched you," said Belle. Then she saw the
look of pain on his face. "I forgot to thank you for
saving my life," she added softly.

The Beast only grunted in reply. But when Belle
turned away, a hint of a smile appeared on his face.

In the days that followed, the Beast tried to be a proper host. He showed Belle his library, and she began to teach him how to act like a gentleman.

"Perhaps it isn't too late," Cogsworth whispered to Mrs. Potts and her son, Chip the teacup. "If Belle could only love the Beast, this dreadful spell might yet be broken."

Before long, Belle thought of the Beast as her dearest friend. And the Beast thought of little but the beautiful Belle.

One night while she was teaching him to dance, the Beast asked, "Belle, are you happy here—with me?"

"Yes," she said without hesitation. But the Beast saw a trace of sadness in her eyes. Then Belle added, "If only I could see my father again, even for a minute."

"You can," the Beast said, handing her the magic mirror.

Belle gazed into it and saw Maurice trudging through the forest. He looked frail and old. As she watched, he collapsed in a heap.

"I must go to him!" Belle cried. "He might be dying!"

"I release you," the Beast said sadly. "But take the mirror. Then you will always have a way to look back and remember me."

With the magic mirror to guide her, Belle soon found her father and brought him home. But their happy reunion was cut short by a pounding on their cottage door. The townspeople had come to take Maurice away.

Gaston's friend LeFou stepped forward. "Maurice has been raving that you were imprisoned by a hideous beast," he said. "Only a crazy man would tell such a tale."

"But it's true," Belle protested. Her worried eyes searched the angry crowd and fell on Gaston. "Gaston!" she cried. "You know my father isn't crazy. Tell them."

Gaston whispered to Belle that he might be able to calm the crowd—if she promised to marry him.

"Never!" Belle exclaimed. "And my father is not crazy. There really is a beast, and I can prove it." She turned to the crowd. "Look in this mirror and see."

The townspeople looked at the Beast in the magic mirror and grew frightened.

"We must hunt down this savage animal!" Gaston cried.

After locking Belle and her father in the cellar of the cottage, the villagers rode off to storm the Beast's castle.

Luckily, little Chip had stowed away in Belle's saddlebag. After the villagers were gone, he used Maurice's latest invention to release Belle and Maurice from the cellar.

By the time Belle reached the castle, the townspeople had broken in. Gaston and the Beast were fighting on the castle roof. The Beast managed to knock Gaston's weapon from his hand. There was nothing to stop him from killing Gaston.

Gaston screamed for mercy, and the Beast turned away from his enemy. Then Belle watched helplessly as Gaston plunged a knife into the Beast's back.

The Beast roared in pain. Backing away from the wounded Beast, Gaston lost his footing and fell off the roof into the fog below.

Belle rushed to the Beast's side.

"You came back," the Beast said weakly. "At least I can see you one last time."

"No! No!" Belle said, sobbing as she kissed his cheek. "Please don't die. . . . I love you."

At that moment the spell was broken. In one magical instant, the Beast turned back into a prince, and the enchanted servants returned to their human forms.

The castle came to life with rejoicing. There was no doubt that the loving couple would live happily ever after.